WHO AM I?

"Where am I from and why am I here?"

A book based on self-identity and purpose.

By

Kevin Munga

Part One "Who am I?"

Part Two - "Where am I from?"

Disclaimer

Family life and Origins

Kevin is the youngest sibling, from a family of three and is of Congolese descent.

Born in Sarcelles, France during 1993, he moved with his family to the United Kingdom in 2003.

PART ONE - "WHO AM I?"

Chapter one ~ The first quarter

"Where did it all start?" Well I am grateful to be on planet earth. That's right! I was due to be aborted when I was a baby. Studies confirmed between 2010 and 2014, the number of abortions were estimated to be around 55.7 million worldwide. In addition, nearly half of those abortions were performed in an unsafe manner. I was born during 1993; I wonder how many abortions were performed that year? "What is my point?"

Prior to my birth, before I had even arrived in to the world, I was already rejected. It is not anyone's fault, my mother was happy that she was pregnant with me. However, she did not know how she would manage taking care of three children whilst residing with her sister in Paris. I had already faced adversity before being brought in to the world, but I am not the only one, some individuals have endured abandonment, others put into care and some discarded in super-markets.

"Is this right?" Of course not, but does it make us less valuable than anyone who started life in abundance, the answer to that question is no. Being born in to wealth and privilege, does not make that person more valuable. BREATHE! It's just a bad start, not a bad life. Pain stays temporarily, but eventually subsides and then comes opportunity following an arising, after the pain. The adversity endured was not meant to break us, its intention was designed for us to break records and "defy the odds;" creating wow-stories and to inspire the world with our testimonies. The pain is a driving force, do not give it power; do not let it maintain a stronghold over you.

The words "I do not want you;" "you are not my son;" "you are not my daughter;" "I cannot have this child right now," and "what do you want from me?" was replaced when **GOD** stepped in. He said, "I do want you;" "you are my son;" "you are my daughter" and "I can have this child right now." Well I guess **GOD** stepped in for me. On the first of May 1993, Kevin Michael Munga was born and my Mother loved me very much. She had only panicked and did not know what God was going to do and I suspect God has stepped in on occasions for you too.

"How do I know this?" Because you are reading this message, there is no greater miracle than a heart-beat; the heart is an indication of hope, grace and blessings. I came in to this world, after a prophesy had been revealed to my Mother. The prophet told her not to worry and stated "God knows why he has given you this child." Every human-being on the planet has a heavenly promise, although admittedly it may not always be immediately apparent.

God knew you were the one that he wanted to send way before you were born. *"Do you believe me?" "Do you sometimes feel as if you are a mistake?"* The unfortunate truth is that more than a million babies die on the day of their birth every year, however, you are still here, alive and breathing, I wonder why? It can only be down to one thing "purpose." Something on this earth necessitates you; your gift, talent and presence.

My Mother and I were talking one evening and she told me, that the day I was born she did not need to purchase a thing and that everything had been bought for me, including diapers, bottles and everything else that was needed, prior to my delivery. My parents had been awarded citizenship a few weeks after my birth and things were looking extremely positive. Sometimes blessings come from situations that cannot be comprehended. My Mother did not know she needed to have me, in order for certain doors to open.

Baby Michael aka Bébé Michel

A year after my birth I was considered a popular baby who gurgled often. My Uncles and Aunts would often cradle play with me, not long after I was nicknamed "Bébé Michel" which is translated as "Baby Michael" in English. Little did I know this nickname would remain with me throughout my childhood. My Mother would share these stories with me and often reminisced that I was very cute and chubby, but an adorable good baby.

At the age of three, I can recall my parents along with two of my older siblings, moving to the commune of Sarcelles in the northern suburbs of Paris. It was a neighbourhood renowned for its high crime and violence. Our neighbours were Senegalese, they were a large family of eight and were very welcoming and our families quickly became acquainted and this is where our introduction as a family began, although it may not appear like much now, trust me where I grew up had a major impact on me. *"What about you?" "Where did you grow up?" "What were your memories?"*

One day my older brother came to collect me from primary school; however on this occasion he was accompanied with his best friend, who was also there to collect his younger brother. I remember it like it was yesterday I was in CP, first year of primary school. Subsequently to this after being collected, my older brother and his friend get in to a heated argument. My brother tells his friend that he will get his little brother to smack me up. At first the comradery began as a joke, but eventually the argument takes a more serious dimension and I realise I am underhandedly being coerced in to having a fight.

Imagine a six-year-old thinking about his first fight, my opponent was aged eight at the time and the two years difference back then meant a lot. Nevertheless, even though I felt the

9

pressure, I couldn't let my brother down it was time to fight. This was about upholding my family's name and reputation. The young kid runs up to me and punches me straight in the face, my cheek instantly turns red. I was in so much shock, I grabbed him and hit him right back. I remember at the time thinking, wow this is my first fight, soon after our older siblings broke up the fight; my brother looks at me and I can tell he is proud of my efforts. On my way home, it dawned on me fighting was the means to prove one's masculinity, but what did I know at the tender age of six?

"What were your first primary experiences? How did you differentiate between right and wrong? Was your example or role model a young person or was it an adult?" I pose these questions because often our past experiences explain some of the ideals that we live by today. Eventually, fighting would become the norm. During CE1, the second year of primary school, I'm involved in my second fight and so on and so forth.

At the age of nine, the trajectory of my life suddenly changes; my mother is diagnosed with Sarcoidosis, a serious condition that can affect many organs within the body, resulting in tumours that can have an adverse effect upon the entire immune system. One evening, my mother decides to move us from Paris to London to join her younger sister Aunt M, for the betterment of her health; it was this transition that ended up changing everything.

Will I ever live with my father again? What about my friends from Sarcelles? I will miss them surely, I guess only time will tell.

Chapter Two ~ Test

Upon our arrival from Paris to London my Mother and two older siblings and I were collected from Waterloo Railway Station. I did my best to take in all the breath-taking views of London's city-life from the side of the car I was seated in. The car journey felt like it was taking forever, eventually we had finally reached our destination and it is nothing like I had expected. As we stepped out of the car, we entered inside a large house and were told by a Pastor my Mother needed to be prayed for. Hours had gone by and we are still in the company of the Pastor's family who resided there.

I remember thinking I really wanted to see Aunt M, the cool Aunt; in my estimation she was one of those ones. Whilst my Mother was being prayed for, it appeared to having little impact and after no improvement; the one day we were expected to remain with the Pastor's family, ended up turning in to an entire week, which I found difficult to comprehend at such an impressionable age. My Mother's eyes were swollen when I was finally able to see her thereafter, the Pastor had mentioned he wanted to speak us, but with me specifically. I remember entering his office and to my unexpected surprise the Pastor's wife was also waiting for me, holding a cane.

"What's going on?" Does this woman believe my Brothers and I are evil? "Is she accusing us of something?" The Pastor's wife had asked me to recall the last dream I had. Maybe due to the unexpectedness of it all and the depraved circumstances I now found myself in, I was unable to instantly recall or answer the question to her satisfaction. The Pastor's wife began hitting me with the cane forcefully, whilst repeating the question "What was the dream you had last night?" "I PROMISE I did not even dream last night." I told her unequivocally. She continues to hit me repeatedly saying that my brothers and I are evil, I desperately needed help. "Mum, where are you?" By now my Mother's illness had taken a stronghold and she was barely responsive. It is almost three o'clock in the morning and I am in tears pleading with God for help.

I remember as a nine year-old wondering whether I would survive to see another day. The Pastor's wife had managed to convince my Mother that we needed to "dry-fast" for three days. I remember seeing the pain in my Mother's eyes, with her health increasingly deteriorating. "Lord have mercy on us," I would often plead, my Mother's health would eventually improve enough, that she was able to find employment as a cleaner. Its pleasing to me, knowing that Mum is finally in a position to be able to buy things for me. Little did I know something awful was about to happen in her absence.

The maltreatment towards my siblings and I occurred whenever my Mum left to go to work. I was often kicked, strangled and sometimes whipped. The heart-wrenching thing about it was there was absolutely no justification for any of it. The only excuse offered was "they" believed we are evil. I was often the only one that was chastised, and the violence was always towards me never my brothers. I suppose he is aware of my vulnerability, due to my age. I was scared to tell my Mother I worried she might actually believe the claims they made about me, so I pray often in the hope that she becomes aware of my plight.

The only break from the maltreatment was attending school. Each time it was home time, I would drag my feet because I was going back to sufferance.

I cry out to God daily; the Pastor says we are not allowed to watch TV and that putting Nutella on bread is considered a luxury. I feel hopeless; this radical transition is so intense and I miss my father desperately. *"Can you recall a time of transitioning in your life; the good and the bad times during the process? "Can you remember how it made you feel?"* The scenario distorted my ideology; I remember thinking ervants of God are considered Angels on earth. However, I acknowledge one's actions should not be used as a means of generalisation upon others.

'aith and prayer

It was time to demonstrate the little faith that I had, so I prayed continuously. I'm overwhelmed with premonitions of my Mother getting better and leaving the place we were staying in and fearfully explaining to her about the abuse I suffered when she was at work. Each time I close my eyes I am able to visualise the sky, it feels as if it's my imagination, but it is a sign from God. A faithful God of signs and wonders. A while later my Mother tells us we are leaving, the Pastor is not in favour of my Mother's decision, but I couldn't be happier; my first test is over. God you are real, but why are you putting me through this?

An area of consideration is 'disruption'; the term within itself means confusion and disorder. The word of God says Joseph was extremely loved by his Father Jacob; Joseph was given a magnificent coat of many colours with beautiful patterns. Additionally, the Bible states Joseph was sold into slavery and his disappearance had been orchestrated by his own brothers. The coat which represented comfortability, love and joy was later soaked in blood. Sometimes comfortability is exchanged for greatness, but this only happens under tested conditions. The word of God tells us subsequently to Joseph being sold as a slave in Egypt; he becomes ruler and a man of power. You may have heard of the saying "God gives his hardest battles to his strongest soldiers." Disruption is development and cause for progress and blossoming, God's tests determine individual elevation.

Chapter three ~ Fresh Start

I questioned our fresh start, is it the start of something beautiful or will it be a nightmare? Mum enrols me in to the local school, Broadmead Primary. It was a class full of characters and within an instant you were able to separate the good pupils from those considered bad. All eyes were on me when the teacher introduced me to my new classmates and I was welcomed by them. The teacher informs them that I can only speak French and the entire class retorts with a unified "ahhh." As a nine year-old it was hard to comprehend the new processes and ways of working. I knew then my future in that class would be subject to how quickly I adapted and acted.

I was intrigued by a particular group (the bad boys), irrespective of how young we were, they had already acquired a sense of awareness and their behaviour was volatile. Without sparing a thought of the consequences, I managed to get acquainted within the group and quickly adapted to the stringent codes of conduct. The group seemed to like me and appealed to my sense of humour, especially during my poor attempts in depicting their Jamaican accents. *"Does this remind you of a time you tried your best to fit in, so you could speak or act in a certain way within the confines of certain groups?"*

I remember how quickly I began to learn English, although there were still periods where I felt isolated. I had been put in to extra language classes for "foreigners" with other Spanish and Portuguese nationals, who encountered little problems in attending them, because they believed their attendance served as a form of respite, from the mainstream curriculum.

I can still remember my first interaction with the opposite sex; it was not the most favourable of experiences. The female in question looked at me and said aggressively "Your Mum;" the comment hurt, I wanted to backhand her as a response to the disrespect she had shown, but my principles and morals prevented me from doing so. From a young age I knew putting my hands on a woman was a "no-no." I never allowed anyone to say anything derogatory about my Mother; she was my world and still is. You could never mention Mummy S in a disrespectful manner without my blood boiling. Little did I know, that little girl would end up becoming my best friend just before starting year seven.

Year seven begins and it's time to make new friends and suss-out who is who. I notice groups quickly being formed, you had your "lady's men", the so-called "bad boys" and "athletes" unfortunately, I did not fit in into any of these groups. Isolation strikes and I barely venture in to the playground. In the coming weeks I start to discover unknown talents I never knew existed and I find myself asking three questions "Who am I?," "Where am I from?" and "Why am I here?" The situation at home is not improving; "I become close friends with a boy in my year group "Frenchy."

Talking with my new friend, reminds me of all the things I am missing back in France. We discuss our "come-ups" and agree to protect and look out for each other. However, it seems like things aren't about to go my way. Frenchy and I are more like brothers than friends and as quickly as our friendship develops, Frenchy is reminded to tell me that he will be changing schools. Why is it that whenever I make a new acquaintance they are suddenly taken away from me? (Shrugs). From that moment, any pain or disappointment I felt remained internal and any perceptions I had about life, regarding its existence I felt implied life ought to be lived alone.

Chapter four ~ The definition of culture

Sarcelles to Croydon

Growing up in Sarcelles (Paris), prior to moving to Croydon in Surrey I found an interesting contrast. I developed my first ideals through learnt behaviour. I remember Sarcelles being a place of solidarity and familiarity; however it was also a violent environment. Many questions arise from the aforementioned terms. *"Is it possible for a place to display aspects of both solidarity and violence when they are polar opposites?"* Underlining issues can often explain the social behaviour of individuals. Tensions rise for various reasons, social deprivation, lack of opportunities and hopelessness whereby, individuals may not be able to identity with revered "role models" from the same environment. Governments have a duty to diversify communities, in order to get the best possible outcomes. However this is not always the case, families on lower incomes are usually housed in similar areas; often resulting in envious and depreciating communities.

How was your experience growing up, do you feel like it characterised your attitude? Environments are powerful and can derive ideologies. The only way to escape this type of torment is to renew and restore the mind in addition to personal development, including the will to becoming more than average. I remember moving from Sarcelles, Paris to Croydon, Surrey as if it was yesterday. It was a diverse multicultural town. Croydon and Sarcelles had lots of similarities in terms of multiculturalism and criminality, however one of the main differentiations were families in Croydon did not appear as impoverished. I believe the violence stems from Government neglect, immoral policing and often the mistreatment of ethnic minorities which primarily fuels tensions.

Police officers employed to patrol urban areas they are unable to relate to causes miscommunication, within communities. Talking from personal experience I can confidently say I had lost count, how many times I had been stopped and searched.

This statement highlights the importance of culture. *What is culture? Where does your culture stem from?* Culture is defined as "ideas, customs, and social behaviour from a particular group of people or society." People do not make culture; in fact it is the reverse. Armed with this intellect, why do individuals choose to align themselves with such negativity? For enhancement, respect, survival, fitting-in or having accessibility to facilities which are not necessarily obtainable in third world countries, where morals and civilisation prevail.

My confusion ends when I see the lack of opportunity in these urban areas; revisiting poignant memories and recalling previous encounters and possibly similar to some of yours. Croydon, Surrey during 2003 in the last year of primary school saw the emergence of many teenage social groups; however the most popular groups accommodated the worst trouble makers. They all spoke the same and shared the same sense of style, but most importantly they all appeared "respected." Some of the perks that came with the come-up and the notoriety included female, identity and security as they abided by their own set of rules. It was not until several years later I realised those dividends were nothing, but mere illusions.

My heritage the Congolese culture is extremely diverse; there is a combination of tradition and influence according to specific regions. Additional influences arrived during the era of colonization; but it had little effect on many of the traditional tribal customs. These customs are authentic from the diet down to the respect bestowed. Admittedly, I find myself caught between, my Congolese heritage and the French/British culture that has been a part of my individuality as an immigrant in the northern suburbs of Paris and to the streets of South London. My background stems from the amazing Democratic Republic of Congo; although I was not born there my Mother ensured I was aware of my history and I learn about the various tribes and the traditional dishes. My Mother often shares fond memories of back home, so I have a clear understanding of what it was like growing up in the Congo. I'm also studying about the various tribes, in particular the four main ones and their specific dialects.

When I make my summary of culture, I get to the conclusion that "Culture often brings people together this translates into love, tradition, respect and solidarity. Culture is often respected and as we know something that respected can convey integrity. However, this love is sometimes contradictory in certain societies as irresponsibility is often tolerable. The solidarity and traditions can at times be diminished, due to the lack of education. Social empowerment and financial resources are responsible for the lack of morality.

Chapter five ~ Choices

Fast-forward to the first year of secondary school my first fight in the playground, brutal. I did not necessarily like fighting, but at the time I felt whatever I allowed would continue, so I fought back, others may refer to it as self-defence. Let's rewind back to a few months before my first fight, this young man, most people called him "Tee." Our first encounter I chased him because he said "your mum" to me. Following the fight, Tee is kicked out of school quite soon after starting, due to his non-compliant behaviour.

He appears to be local to the area, sometimes we see each other and whenever we do he grins and taunts me calling out "Kevin Munga." I ignore him and continue to turn a blind eye, until one day I over hear someone suggest, "If Tee gets arrested, he'll say his name is Kevin Munga." Fuelled by the implication my blood boils, but I act like I'm oblivious to the claims. I try to keep my composure and decide to investigate the allegations when I can. I will return to Tee later, but for now I want to raise some of the other issues that arose. Secondary school was not really the best experience, however I did make a very close friend CH and I'm interested to see how our friendship develops in the future.

Aged sixteen and at College now, it's time to get away from seeing the same faces. I start my first day at Coulsdon College which is thirty minutes away from Croydon. I enter the college with a huge smile on my face, which was quickly removed when I hear someone say "Kevin Munga" in an aggressive tone, its Tee. I look at him then immediately look away; thinking about my objective to get my head down and focus on my studies, without having to worry about anyone causing me problems. How can I achieve this with Tee in the same facility as me? Realising things for what they were, I decide to avoid him as much as possible. *Can*

I do my best to avoid him, but he is in the common room cafeteria and I can feel his eyes fixated on me. I have an internal conversation with myself. "Kevin just keep your head down and do not get yourself kicked out, Tee is not worth it." The tension is immense we are in the external recreational area; Tee maintains his focus on me and my group of friends. As the tensions rise among the two groups, the issue is no longer an isolated problem anymore between two people.

Tee confronts our group with his friends and queries whether there's a problem. We all reply simultaneously "There isn't one" and we call them out as the perpetrators who had been studying us. Tee begins to giggle and reminds us they're not children anymore and that if we wanted trouble, he would give us what we were looking for. We attempt to ignore him, but eventually end up arguing. The arguments die down after a while and one of the members of his group suggest they retreat. Several weeks after the incident, I settle back in to regular life; at times I still see Tee eyeing me, which I find very frustrating.

Encounter with Tee

It's the day of the talent show, an auspicious occasion; as I prepare for my act, I am nervous so I head outside for some fresh air. I notice Tee in the corridor, he begins singing a song making innuendos and insults me. I'm unable to contain my anger any longer, majorly upset I resort to challenging whether he is talking to me. He looks at me with a sneaky grin and retorts "Yeah." I ask him if he has a problem, however deep down I know that this can be avoided. I check myself, "Kevin what are you doing?" I'm equipped for whatever is about to happen next. Tee threatens to slice my face and shouts out "THIS IS MY COLLEGE!" I'm undeterred there's no fear in my eyes, I am ready for whatever is about to happen, I respond "Do it then."

To my surprise Tee begins to back down and quickly diffuses the situation and I walk away in an attempt to calm down and clear my mind ahead of the performance. As I ventured back inside the college Tee yells out "You're manned up now yeah, say nothing." I hadn't seen Tee again since the incident, but I have heard from friends that he was later incarcerated; I wish him all the best,

You remember my close friend CH? Well CH ended up in the same predicament as me. He attended Coulsdon College and attempted to keep his head down, however trouble just seems to find us, but we have each other's back if there's ever a problem. We were just teenagers who enjoyed having a laugh and play fighting. On one occasion at college we heard rumours about one CH's old affiliations who was said to want retribution. What do I mean by that? The people that were coming for CH believe he is from a particular gang, due to his acquaintances. Previously, I stated if CH is in trouble, I would have no choice but to become involved.

We get word his rivals are intending on coming for him the following day; that day is a day I'll never forget. CH is wearing a stab-proofed vest, seeing him dressed in that way, gave me the chills. We were only sixteen and were focused on completing our studies. How is it I've been threatened with being stabbed in the face and my best friend has to attend college in a stab proofed vest? I remember our last conversation before CH entered his class, "I am only wearing a stab proofed vest, what If they come with a gun?" I responded, "The vest will be of little protection," don't worry you are my brother and I'm here for you. We were both feeling reticent as we departed to our classes.

At the end of College, we contemplate various options from jumping the barriers to getting the train, because it was less risky than taking the bus or just accepting our fates. As we leave college, an older guy is waiting outside holding a metal bar and we are grateful for protection on offer. By God's Grace no one else is present; we decide to make a run for it because we needed to get away. I remember getting home and messaging CH, "Today was a mad day Bro" and CH messages back "I know, I suspect there will more days like these".

Group of 4

We meet up with JB and TY at College, now there are four of us in the group. As teenagers our only interests are to make a few quid legitimately and play football, all the normal things teenagers would do. On one occasion we head to an area in South London called Crystal Palace, I cannot recall whose idea it was to go there. We saw a shop in the area; CH was far from economical and always spending his money on silly things. Upon entering the store there were up to fifteen young men waiting outside the entrance. I remember thinking can't we even visit another area in peace.

One of the men confronts us and inquires where we are from. CH responds to him, but JB and I ignore him. "How dare he? Does he own the area?" I say to myself, CH tells them we're from the area. The group appear doubtful of the answers they had been supplied and some of the others in the group begin shouting at us that we were mad. There was an elder person also standing outside the shop, who told the offenders to leave us alone, he was keen for them to leave the location, due to wanting to remain inconspicuous as he tended to some illegal matters of his own.

The group draws near and inform us they need to tax us for coming to the area and demand ten pounds from each of us. JB almost burst out laughing, contemplating whether the ransom demand had been genuine. We told them they wouldn't be getting a penny from us, the older guy interrupts the proceedings and tells the offenders if they refuse to move on, he would become really angry and bellows at them to move instantly. The main culprit in the group kisses his teeth and the group leaves. We kept watching our backs whilst we remained in the area; the whole incident was surreal, if I am honest. London is a city where you have to think twice when visiting other areas.

Beat them or join them

As a sixteen year old the vast variety of options available can be considered extreme. The rational part of a teen's brain is not fully developed and won't be, until at least the age of twenty-five. *Can you just imagine the radical thoughts I would have experienced at the time?* According to research completed at the University of Rochester studies show adult and teenaged brains work differently. Adults think with the prefrontal cortex, which is stimulated by the rational part of the brain. This is the part of the brain that responds to situations with good judgment and an awareness of long-term consequences. The teenaged brain processes information with the amygdala, this is the emotional stimulus.

In teenaged brains, the connections between the emotional and the decision-making are still in development, however this is not always at the same rate. That's the reason teenagers can experience an overwhelming amount of emotional involvement. Some teenagers experience difficulty attempting to explain what they may have been thinking at the time and studies show they are likely to have been "feeling" more than they were actually "thinking."

Acting off emotions I begin to contemplate and I message CH to ask his opinion, "I don't know about you bro, but I am getting tired of this life. It feels as if we are victims to a system that has been put in place, because we're not part of a gang." CH asks "What are you saying?" "Bro I am saying it feels like if you can't beat them then you have to join them." CH retorts "Say nothing let me speak to Kay, let's arrange to meet these so called gangsters next week." I did not know what to expect, my associates were in to football and hanging around the chicken shop. I was confused about what being in a gang meant.

During the earlier discussion they had asked if we made music. I loved rapping and I confirmed I did. I had started rapping when I was little; the group were interested in my ability to rap and assumed we were affiliates. Finding the balance between attending lessons and teenaged life was challenging. On one occasion I missed my last lesson for a fight, this resulted in changing my character from who I used to be, a law abiding citizen. "Drillz" was my nickname now, it has always been, but now the intention is to make my name notorious on the streets. I'm regularly told about fights in the area, those times often stood out to me. For example, the time we woke up at seven in the morning to beat someone up, or another occasion just five of us went to fight an entire school.

This was not the life I intended, but I refused to be a victim of my life's circumstances any further. My Mother's health is deteriorating; I miss my father and my brothers. I am able to meet with them occasionally, but living apart from them just isn't the same. I was looking forward to our impending trip to Paris in the summer, my friend TY sent me a picture of a young man who had died over the weekend. I was shocked when I heard about the incident, I asked TY about what had happened and he said the man had died, due to gang violence. TY had known the person; the young victim was a student at his school, which made it even more apparent about how detrimental life was on the streets.

People were dying for no reason and this would be a wake-up call for many. I thank God I am in Paris and recognise that tensions in the local area would be at their most heightened. I decide it's time to make some life choices, CH and I semi-retreat from the street scene; the impact of the incident had an overwhelming calming effect in the area. I have had to fight my entire life when required, but people are actually dying from living a street life. I remember CH having to wear a stab-proof vest, in order to protect himself, just to go college that's how serious life had become. I thought about all the times I had become embroiled in group fights, the pent up adrenalin which made my heart beat erratically. The sworn enemies who chased me and the times I happened to be the perpetrator, these incidents became the norm, whereby no serious repercussions were ever expected, provided there were no weapons involved, however not everyone lived by the same street principles.

At times our choices can be selfish; I even started to believe the hype and notoriety that came with my new found popularity, without thinking of the consequences, should anything sinister happen to me. It wouldn't impact the local community only my family, whilst everyone else would continue their lives. *"When you make a decision who else does it affect? Furthermore, does it affect yourself, your family and possibly your eternity?"* It was time to make some lifetime decisions. These days I am not that street anymore. I haven't seen my old friends, "ridden out" or gone to a fight in a long time, maybe I should put all my efforts in to making music. As I focus on doing so, I still find myself being dragged in to my friend's problems, and often have to ask myself whether it's worth it. At the age of eighteen I feel like I have become a by-product of my environment, *"What makes me say that?"* All of my faith and ideologies stem from ideas and beliefs that have been indoctrinated as part of my growing up.

Big cars, jewellery, designer clothing, are a symbol of wealth in my community and without them I am made to feel as if I am unworthy. I feel an underlying pressure to begin acquiring such possessions and to do so, making money becomes the motivation. I met someone in college who had recognised me from a music video, he makes money on the streets and I wonder if he can bring me in. He propositions me about making some money, but I'm somewhat undecided. I was already making money of my own on the roads, but all I had to show for it was clothes and material gain, none of it was meaningful. I had no savings; future plans or direction and quickly came to the realisation that progression is restricted with illegal gains. "When will Kevin start to make the right choices?"

My mother was always inviting me to church, but her place of worship never appealed to me. There was one occasion she insisted on me accompanying her; because it was an important meeting and I could tell it would mean everything to her. I relented and told her I would meet her there. The trains were taking forever and the delays made it feel like it was a sign from God, eventually all the trains were cancelled and I had to find an alternative route to get there, especially as Mum had emphasised how important it was for me to attend. I had dressed appropriately for the occasion in my G-star jeans that I had tucked in to my socks with a G-star jacket, and black Air Forces. To complete the look I wore a watch and a pinky ring. I felt like I was dressed the part as I walk through the flats towards the church.

In the distance, I saw a group of individuals that I paid little attention to, however I should not have been so careless. There were approximately fifteen youths on pushbikes; a young girl nearby has a sincere look of concern etched upon her face, it was as if she feared something sinister might happen to me. As I walk past the group, I could hear the sounds of footsteps running up behind me, someone from the group shouts out "Oi". I'm not scared, but I'm expecting a confrontation and respond to the call. A boy from the group begins asking where I'm from. The scenario occurs in exactly the same way as previous occasions, although I'm in North London and from South London, I extend the truth and state I'm from North.

The group accuse me of lying to them, one of the youths makes an attempt to steal my watch and whilst I defend myself

I'm punched and tackled. Whilst grappling with the perpetrators my phone escapes from my pocket and falls on the ground, someone from the group takes it and runs off. Then I hear someone from the group mention they didn't like my attitude, merely because I was defending myself. He asks one of the others to hand him a knife..."WHERE'S THE KNIFE?" I visualise eighteen years of my life flash before me. "Lord help me out of this situation." I kept thinking if I don't get stabbed in the chest, I have every chance of survival. I said a soft prayer to myself, suddenly after asking for the knife I quickly look into the direction I had been walking in. Then without warning I break free from their grasp and they run into the opposite direction. By God's grace I only sustain a broken nose and a little dented pride as a result of that incident. Thank God I had made it alive and was able to live to see another day.

As I made off from the scene I kept thinking about retaliation. Later, I got a female to message the new owner of my phone and discovered it had been sold to someone through an app called BBM. She had even gone to the length of arranging a meeting with him so I could extort my revenge, but during the ordeal the girl mentioned the torture she wanted extracted on him. The intended victim became paranoid and inquired with the girl whether she had any intentions of setting him up and made it clear he was not responsible for how the phone had been acquired, whilst maintaining his only accountability was that he had inherited the device legitimately. As a God fearing person, I realised in that moment that God's revenge is just and the best course of action in that situation was to leave it in God's Hands, to deal with.

1 Peter 3:9

Do not repay evil with evil or insult with insult. On the contrary, repay evil with blessings, because to this you were called so that you may inherit a blessing.

A conversation with God: "You made the right choice Kevin, you may not have been innocent all your life..." but something extremely special happened to me the following year. I was now nineteen and had been invited to church by some old friends, whom I used to get up to no good with in the streets as a teenager, but had since turned their lives over to Christ. I had left the street life, but doing so had not brought me closer to God.

A poignant moment for me during the church service was witnessing my friend in tears at the altar as he presented his testimony. He felt relieved and grateful that God granted him an acquittal during his court trial. He explained that he had been destined to go to jail for a very long time, but had promised his mother if he was found not guilty, he would devote the rest of his life to serving God. I witnessed God in His Glory in that moment when my friend was found not guilty for a knife possession charge and as a result, the friend in question has not looked back since. That particular day was amazing; I witnessed that transition was attainable and also a possibility for me.

I remember closing my eyes and soon after instantly standing upright on my feet. I was certain the Holy Spirit had come over me and from there, a new life had begun for me and I became a Born-Again Christian. For a brief moment I questioned my decision, regarding the new life I had undertaken. "Kevin, do you know what this journey will mean?" I asked myself, as I dwelled upon my inhibitions, I then heard the Lord say to me "No my Son, this new path you are taking, means you are free now."

- Discipline is not restriction it is freedom.

Chapter six ~ Use your disadvantage to your advantage

How can you have a testimony without the test?

I have given my life to Christ, but does that make me adequate and efficient? With much enthusiasm I attend church as often as possible, but before moving on to that, I will explain how I was able to evolve as an Individual and create sustainability. I finished school with just one GCSE in French, and that was only because it was my native language, if I'm brutally honest.

I managed to scrape through college with a triple pass; I am nineteen and interested in attending University, but wonder whether my qualifications are good enough to be accepted. Eventually, I made the decision to apply for a low ranking university, my toughest battle was deciding on which course to study. My Mother's friend believes academia may not be my forte, but I decide to try a business course in the belief it will create more opportunities.

I remember walking into my first lecture I called my mum as always. "Maman, Maman j'etait dans l'auditorium je suis a l'université maintenant." Translated in to English "Mum, Mum I am in the lecture room." *"What was your educational background like, did you excel in school and was it an enjoyable experience?"* Something tells me university is similar to college, so I begin missing classes and stop attending and don't take it seriously. I made friends with a girl in Uni and for the purposes of infringement and privacy laws, I will refer to her as "Bee."

Bee would tear stripes of me regularly, unimpressed with my lack of focus and purpose. She repeatedly tried to reason with me about avoiding the pitfalls of life, most other young black males were getting caught up in. Her advice was like talking to a brick wall and would often go in one ear and straight out of the other, often feeling as if I was being judged. I remained stuck in my ways, life carried on as usual and I continued attending lectures late and had misplaced my drive and ambition. What Bee failed to realise was that I struggled with understanding why education was so important.

I cannot recall an occasion whereby a teacher bothered to notice the difficulties I experienced during my studies or why I was failing as a student or whether there were any personal issues that had attributed to my lack of progress. Fast forward to the end of the year and I had failed all the modules I had taken, barring one. To be honest I do not know what I expected, kept hearing my inner voice telling me "You must reap what you sow." This time I took the loss personally and constantly berated myself, "Kevin, You messed up again; you actually had an opportunity to make it right, but now it's back to square one;" I used my misfortune to reach out to God. "I have you Lord, but how will I make it out of this situation. I have no education and I'm unemployed, what do I do next?"

Something at the back of my mind convinces me, this could be a good thing, because I never really wanted to go to university anyways and my reason for attending was more about something to do. I began job hunting, after registering with an agency. However, every job interview I attend is unsuccessful. My life feels as if it is at a standstill. *"Have you ever felt like that before?"* My mind was telling me to do the responsible thing and sign-up at the Job Centre, but my pride was telling me the opposite. Maann! I was beginning to feel like a complete failure; being from the "Ends" where I was from, whilst signing-on at the Job Centre, I felt was humiliating.

I had to face facts; maybe this was the start of the humbling process for me, with few options available I sign on to the Job Centre and begin receiving state benefits of two hundred and fifty pounds monthly, just enough to pay for my mobile phone contract, food and a travel card. I went from wanting the finest things in life to feeling like nothing. *"Have you ever had a similar humbling experience?"* Later that week I went to meet a close friend of mine JB. I first referred to JB, previously in Chapter Five. JB is unaware of the benefit payments I had been receiving; I felt too embarrassed to tell him I had been signing-on. But JB had already noticed the paperwork poking out of my pocket and when we spoke later that week, he said "Brother if you are going to hide your signing-on papers, at least do a good job, because I can see the paperwork hanging out of your pocket."

I just had to laugh, it goes to show how stressed I was, having made so much effort trying to hide what was really going on and unbeknown to me JB had ended up seeing the evidence anyway. Despite the setbacks, I continued attending job interviews without much success. I remember asking God one morning "Why do you actually wake me up?" During the next appointment at the Job Centre I realised as a twenty year-old; I constantly compared myself to my peers; most were already driving and in their second year of University.

Unknowingly comparing yourself to anyone else is the worst mistake you could ever make. Success should only be compared to what you could have achieved. I had attempted at becoming a security guard, but I quickly lost the enthusiasm for it and knew deep down it was not what I saw myself aspiring to, but I felt a strong desire to serve and help people in some way. *"Have you ever felt like that before?"* In discovering your purpose, you can often be found doing something completely different, just for the sake of saying "I do something."

Commuting by train one day, I noticed an advertisement offering Access courses. For a moment, I interpret the discovery as a possible golden opportunity. The Access course was an intensive programme that enabled you to enter University upon completion. I noted the details and later made contact regarding their business courses and prices. I remember asking my Mother for half of the money to pay for the course and the other funds my brother kindly provided. Surprisingly my application was successful and the course moderator confirmed I was to start an Access to Law course in January.

Law! I thought there must have been a mistake; however the course coordinator reconfirmed I had been accepted on to the course; sensing my shock she inquired whether there was an issue. I placed the phone receiver down; I urgently needed to speak with my mum. "Maman I doubt I will be able to do Law, I failed when I went to University last time, how could I succeed at doing Law?" My mother responded "Son you can do anything you put your mind to." I just remember thinking to myself surely this is not a mistake or coincidence, God must want me to do this, in the end everything worked out accordingly and I successfully completed the Law Access course. Sometimes courage is required; the definition of courage "Is the ability to start something, without the guarantee of success." I remember thinking if Kevin went from just having one GCSE to a Law degree imagine that, it was possible to have limited education to graduating such a prestigious course. My disadvantage had the potential to become my advantage and an inspirational story for others one day.

Chapter seven ~ Epiphany

I start my Access to Law course, despite my father's misgivings. He questioned whether I was sure about doing the course. "Reading is a pivotal part of the course son and I know you don't read much." He said. I told him not to worry and confidently stated I would be able to complete the course successfully. At that moment, I realised how much I needed to succeed and how much my experience could help other individuals whose stories where similar to mine, if I triumphed. January arrives and the course starts I dedicate most of my time and effort and its taking everything out of me literally blood, sweat and tears. I am the first person in the library and the last to leave. At that moment, my life consists of only church and university, hence the title of this chapter "Epiphany".

An epiphany is depicted as "A moment of sudden and great revelation or realisation." From a Christian stand point it is translated as "A manifestation of Christ to the Gentiles as represented by the Magi." The Magi's, were wise men that followed a miraculous guiding star to Bethlehem, where they paid homage to the infant Jesus as King (Matthew 2:1-12). Just like my situation when Christ stepped in I followed his path, similar to following the guiding star. My life began to make a lot more sense, I was apparently smarter than my peers who often remarked that I was years ahead of my time and wiser beyond my years, those compliments was 'firsts' for me.

I would attend networking events and bought myself a new suit to look the part. Nevertheless, I had no idea that through progress I would still encounter adversity. Inky Johnson says "You either come out of adversity, or you are in the midst of it." Irrespective of any progress made, the risk of adversity is always possible, so stay prepared. The hardest times of your life often lead to the greatest times. It's "Results Day," I had submitted some coursework and was expecting an amazing mark. I received a mark of forty-seven percent and was one of the only pupils who had passed in the class. I cannot explain the feeling, because it was new to me. I had begun transitioning from the losing side to the winning side. I had actually passed something related to my education, wow. Subsequently, I consistently passed every exam, until I hit a brick wall. I had encountered adversity and I felt unprepared for what may happen.

Jim Rohn states "How quickly and responsibly we react to adversity, is far more important than the adversity itself." Additionally, Inky Johnson says "You do not rise to the adversity; you revert back to your training." It was another obstacle, because it felt so good to be an achiever and within that moment I felt like a failure all over again, without realising all successful men failed and that even if I failed ninety-nine times all I needed was to succeed once. I started reflecting on my life, I had failed an entire portfolio on my Access course, which delayed starting my Degree to September instead of May.

I remember it like it was yesterday, for once I had panicked I actually cared that I had failed an assignment. I realised that I had become content, because I was focused on the success rather than my studies. This was the reason for my consequence, for a moment I felt I had returned to square one and felt really down about it and it started to over consume me. During church the Pastor talked about suicide, to be honest I felt like he was talking directly to me, I had enough. I knew I had to stop feeling sorry for myself, I had the potential and capability so decided to attempt the portfolio again.

I dedicated more time to my portfolio the second time around and started to see positive results from what had been a negative situation. I had three months to prepare for September and I had started to feel more positive about things. I remember going to the examiner's office with my portfolio. Praying I had got it right this time, the Examiner was unable to confirm how well I had faired, because it was against the rules, however, she told me to relax and stated my final mark was in the safe zone. I left the office knowing I had done well enough to pass and happy I would be studying Law in September.

PART TWO – "WHERE AM I FROM?"

Chapter eight ~ Wake-up call

Where am I from? Whilst getting back in to my stride I receive a huge wake-up call. I was preparing to start the Law degree when I received a Facebook message from AL a childhood friend of mine that another childhood friend bearing the same name "AL" had died. To clarify I had two childhood friends with the same name "AL" and they were my neighbours. We had all lived in the same block and grew up together, getting up to mischief and doing what young kids normally do, including playing "Knockdown Ginger" and football together. AL's death shook me; I was in attendance at a church service when I was notified about it. Fighting back the tears as the church service concluded, I hid in a corner.

He repeats AL is dead!! He was stabbed with a pointy object that afternoon and the instrument had pierced his heart. I felt sick to my stomach and still do to this day. He told me that MO was with him and had ended up in a coma. MO, another friend also lived in the same block as us and was considered a good friend. I shouted "What happened to MO?" AL stated he had been stabbed in the stomach. I wiped away my tears and recalled a flashback moment, I thought about the memories we had shared with AL he was only seventeen years old. "Lord why?" I couldn't comprehend that the life of such an amazing individual had been taken at such an impressionable age; in an instant I was beginning to view life for what it really was.

Memories with AL

AL was amazing and I am not just saying this because of his death. I remember one morning my cousin from Neuilly-Sur-Marne a town in Paris came to visit. As we went out to play AL told us to come to his party. As we began getting ready, because we had heard the word party we thought surely we need to look Dapper for the event. Lucky for me I already had a haircut, my older brother suggested that he should cut my cousin's hair "ahhh" man, I was thinking my cousins brave for letting that happen. Laugh out loud the hair clipper had stopped working whilst my brother was cutting his hair. My brother looked at me, I looked at my cousin; we knew what time it was.

My cousin had received half a haircut and was fuming; in the end he borrowed one of my brother's hats. I looked at him and laughed a little you can understand that this was quite a comedic moment, although my cousin was not amused, we went to the party we were kids approximately eleven years old. We danced and played video games then suddenly AL snatched my cousin's hat off his head. My cousin was upset and quickly grabbed the hat back; I had to prevent myself from laughing. When I think of AL its memories like these that break my heart. Another memory was when he used to call me chubby. AL was a cheeky guy I chased him all the way to his house, I laugh when I think of it now and I will forever miss him.

After his death there was immense tension the entire neighbourhood wanted to avenge his death. Those that had witnessed the incident wanted to retaliate. It took the 'olders' (the older lot) to calm everyone down appealing to the community that they did not need a blood bath. Pleading with the younger lot telling them "We understand your pain but please if you live by the gun you will die by the gun." I guess the olders were right revenge is God's. AL's killer was given ten years of jail time not enough in my eyes in that moment. Nevertheless, the family said they were just happy justice was served. The reason for the lenient sentence was because the killer was a minor at the time of the crime.

Chapter nine ~ Product of our environment

I returned to the area several months after AL's murder. As I stood in front of his block of flats I felt goose bumps; I was unable to attend AL's funeral, I was in too much pain to do so. The flats weren't the same anymore and till this day it still feels weird whenever I walk past his house; Sarcelles, Sablons will never feel the same. MO had ended up in a mental institution, following his recovery, I found it difficult to accept his demise; the entire incident had a devastating effect on him. At the time of AL's murder MO was only sixteen years of age. He awoke from a coma to learning his best friend had died, shortly after he was also incarcerated. The mental institution was the third tragic thing that happened to him can you imagine that? Then I heard the devastating news that MO committed suicide heart-broken. What about my neighbour from across the corridor who has the same name as me. I used to go to his house if my parents weren't back from work; unfortunately he had also ended up in jail.

My ends were becoming a product of our environment? *"Is it just death or jail?"* Rapper Kery James states "Us behind bars, them in the Senate they defend their interests, elude us of our problems, but a question remains unanswered. What have we done for ourselves? What have we done to protect our people? Look what is becoming of our little brothers? Firstly, its failure in education, marginalisation then anger which leads to violence, jail and ultimately the graveyard. We're not condemned to failure, it is true that for us it is hard, but it should not become a pretext"

According to sociologist Didier Fass in the under representation of ethics in France is demonstrated by looking at its social class. In 2007, Sociologists Veronique le Goaziou and Laurent Mucchielli found files dealing with the incarceration of the under eighteen of Versailles. The conclusion found two thirds of the incarcerated youth were minorities, but aside from that these people came predominately from deprived areas. However, the system that is aware of this pattern chooses to ignore it and does not intervene, in the hope of never changing the process. I find it disheartening, knowing the statistics are often highlighted to fuel fear, instead of raising awareness and helping. This is the push instilled in becoming a "product of our own environment".

Prior to AL's death another person in the neighbourhood had died, although he had died from natural causes, we were still on edge. Looking back at MO's circumstances, being stabbed in the stomach and ending up incarcerated, prior to being sent to a mental institution. *How do we not become products of our environment?* What had gone wrong? We were just kids and not too long ago we would have been outside either playing football or chase. Many youths from the neighbourhood had been incarcerated, including a family member of mine.

The labels of "Banlieusard;" the English interpretation "Hoodlum" were on the horizon. The revelation appeared to be a system in place, whereby we were expected to become by-products of our social economic conditions. My older brother YV had recently graduated from his studies and had become an Engineer. During interviews his employers were often impressed that he came from Sarcelles and recognised it as a rarity for someone from that part of the world to succeed in the profession as he had. You can just imagine how many subliminal limitations there are, especially when entering certain professions that do not cater to us. Having to face the odds and told repeatedly you are unsuccessful following every interview you attend. *"How do we beat the system?"* Sometimes it may be necessary to create an opportunity that you are destined to be a part of.

Maybe it doesn't mean because we are from Sarcelles we can only enter low-tier professions it's just a mind-set that makes us believe this is all we are good for.

"Sometimes you've got to create what you want to be a part of."

Chapter ten ~ If I want it then maybe I have to create it

My mission commences, *"Why are we all at mediocre levels, when we are from the same depraved localities?* **Aged** just twenty-one I tell a friend I am embarking on my journey in becoming a law practitioner. Trying to challenge the ideology, that in order to become a somebody where I am from, you need road status. And the only way young black males make it where I am from is if they know how to kick a ball or write lyrics. I will fight to show progressive intellectuals that we can make it within deprived areas. Sarcelles, Villiers le Bel, Croydon, Peckham, Harlem and the list goes on, irrespective of your external make up, it should not define your intellect.

Why should your appearance be intertwined with your character? **This had** become my mission, sometimes I felt down and there were times it felt I was fighting a losing battle. Soon after I was approached by an individual who told me something I would never forget. "Kevin, the fact that you are studying Law is already proof you are more than just average, you just need to make other people believe it, but in order for that to happen, you need to succeed."

I started to believe my mission was no longer just mine, but a mission for all of us. What if reading became "cool" other than just intellectualism? I was so happy because I knew this was the beginning of my campaign. I began volunteering at a church called New Life Christian Centre. My aim is to help a world that is in need of help, from a world of distorted ideologies, confused and bound by pain and sorrow of the streets. I find myself situated on the other side of the street, but can certainly relate to it.

Activism

On my journey of activism I decided to research the leaders that I believed I could relate to, in terms of the positive changes they attempted to implement. I knew I wanted to emulate Martin Luther King Jr. and began researching his ideologies. Martin Luther King Jr. had suffered many adversities as a result of his beliefs, yet his non-violent approach allowed me to identify with him as a Leader. Going forward there would be occasions whereby I may risk offending others in my pursuit of bringing about change, however in order to obtain it, I knew I had to risk offending. Dr. King's bravery and courage became more than an inspiration to me.

Martin Luther King Jr. - Misfortunes

Martin Luther King Jr was arrested and jailed more than twenty times.

- In 1956 his life and family was threatened in the bombing of his home.

- In 1958 Dr. King was stabbed with a letter opener during a book signing.

- In 1968 it was his assassination, he had faith and so much confidence and I was inspired.

According to (Britannica, 2020)

We lived in different times nevertheless struggle is universal and even though times have changed I have the blueprint of someone that was able to create change. Activism started with conversations I would often hear people saying Kevin you need to write a book. I used to think a whole book? How will I be able to achieve that? I kept reposting black empowering posts on Instagram with the hashtag #youngblackmaleshavepotential. At the back of my mind I knew that a book was my true calling. I couldn't ignore the compulsion I knew God was speaking to me. I just remember asking myself how I will get these chapters completed. Organically I started writing the first chapter gangsterism, the second one about black on black crime and so on and so forth. Whoever is of God hears the word of God. The reason why you do not hear them is that you are not of God" John.8.47.

I automatically realised the closer I was to God the more I would hear him. I had listened to him and here I was writing the final chapter "Faith and a fighting spirit". It was all done but I was not sure about the quality, anyways it's in God's hands now I am about to launch it. A day before my book launches I have a dream that my book is monumental and in my dream funnily enough Martin Luther King features on the front page. As I open the book I see red writing like the way it's written in the bible when Jesus is speaking. I hear an authoritative voice say to me I have replaced your words with mine. And I see the words written in black writing crossed out. I hear the same voice saying release the book, the following day on 2nd October 2017 a copy of "Young Black Males Have Potential" was delivered in the post.

I had various reasons for writing the book, breaking a system, stigmas, stereotypes, toxic masculinity and gangsterism. Nevertheless, if I had to narrow it down to the two most important reasons, I would say I was trying to create the role model that I wish I had growing up. By becoming an author I knew I could create an alternative for a young man growing up in the inner city of London. My second most important reason was reaching members of parliament. I knew the only way to get a seat at the table and discuss our issues was if I wrote a book. It is a formal format and I knew I could potentially meet Head of States this way within the UK as a short term goal and internationally as a long term goal.

Chapter eleven ~ Misunderstood & wrongfully judged

Immorally judged as I make my introduction in to the corporate world, I notice the stares. I enter Eversheds one of the top ten leading Law firms within the UK. My smile seems to make me stand out; I question whether it's a positive thing or is it just my gold tooth that's making my appearance more prominent. I am there on placement for a week. I'm aware a good placement can be a life changing experience. I am there on a mission-break in addition, with the stigma of "a hood boy," due to my attire and gold tooth. Furthermore, what is an "intellectual?" someone who wears a pair of glasses and a suit.

Well here is my answer for those that can relate. "To the streets, don't think for a second reading is long, it saved my life and to the people that judged me, don't think for one second intellectualism comes with a certain image. Don't assume the man who wears a suit is educated, yet the man who has a gold tooth and wears a leather jacket is uneducated. Imagine being able to change the narrative; imagine young men from deprived areas acquiring knowledge, being well-spoken and leading others in years to come. Imagine the mandem armed with intellectual weaponry, I'm not referring to institutionalised education; its way more than that, the application of knowledge can provide healing.

I wrote this message to the wrongly accused and the misunderstood. It's down to us to change the narrative, why not have Oxford graduates with dreadlocks and lawyers with gold teeth, *"does it really matter?"* The only element of importance worth considering is the content of one's character. Can you really assume that a lady is unprofessional because of her naturally curly hair? Or the unshaven man; does not mean he is unworthy of the role he has applied for. This narrative needs to change and it will. Those perceived as hoodlums will become future bankers, lawyers and the deepest philosophers of our generation. Let's continue becoming educated, qualified and lastly lets carry on being ourselves because whether they like it or not we will rise to the top, if we can convince our intellects to do so.

PART THREE – "WHY AM I HERE?"

Chapter twelve - The content of character

"Why do you live a selective lifestyle?" This chapter highlights the gravity and severity of our decisions. I live according to a quote that I have written. Inspired by, the great Dr Myles Munroe, "Decisions become easy when you can live with the consequences." I believe this quote refers to weighing-up the results, including many questions that are unanswered. For example, *is it worth it? Will I benefit from it? Will I be able to live with it?* I have made some poor decisions in my life, but let's look at some of the purposes that I now live by. I made the decision not to drink alcohol. I don't enjoy the taste of alcohol, but the facts remain from the moment I knew my purpose, I had researched the detrimental effects of drinking and concluded it was something that would not be of interest to me.

I knew that alcohol could cause vision and hearing impairments, including affecting speech and coordination. Alcohol can affect judgement and self-control and can cause one to act differently when inebriated, in comparison to normal behaviour and it is impossible to make the best judgements, whilst under the influence. *"How do you cope when most people around you drink?"* My response to that is "The average man adheres to what is glorified and glamorised around him," *(Kevin Munga).*

"Why have you chosen to follow Christ and have faith?" I recognised I was travelling through life with no direction and without principals. From the lessons I had learnt during my upbringing, I knew I needed discipleship. These are formed from the Ten Commandments; they derive all my ideals and the relationships I maintain.

Love and relationships

We tend to always look at side (A), forgetting that side (B) exists; everything has a time for it to manifest. You do not need to rush relationships; you need to wait on for your God given wife/husband. Many of us say we want a partner, *but what is your prayer, and most importantly what is your conduct?* A destructive phrase used by many women from the Twenty-First century "Men are trash."

However, if this is the case, then women must be the wastebin, like my friend RH always says. When you allow that man to be with you, what does that say about you? Even if it was a part of your past, I am often asked why I don't listen to music I cannot learn from? Music has the power to inspire and entertain, however it also has the powerful psychological effect that can improve your health and well-being. Instead of thinking of music as entertainment, consider some of the major health benefits one could gain if you were to listen to music that caused upliftment. The idea that music can influence your thoughts, feelings and behaviours probably does not come as much of a surprise. The psychological effects of music can be powerful and wide-ranging. Nevertheless, it is somewhat responsible for evoking a range of emotions.

The content of character "Kevin why are you so mindful of your reputation?" Because my reputation means everything to me, integrity is defined as a state of being whole and undivided, the quality of honesty. The ability to have strong morals strong principles, if I am called to be Leader integrity is paramount. The word integrity is associated to uprightness, probity, rectitude and honour. I can't just teach it, I know I have to exemplify it, sometimes the sermon you need to preach is your lifestyle.

Chapter thirteen ~ Passion

After successfully completing my placement at Eversheds I began to realise my purpose on earth. I had a lot of unanswered questions. Wikipedia was my go to place for the greats, but how do I become great? I loved reading their stories and seeing their struggles and I would see some of the many hurdles they had to face. Inadequacy at school, poverty, domestic abuse, drugs, emotional abuse. Disabilities, unemployment and homelessness but however they were still able to turn their pain into positivity.

I wanted to pour my efforts into my community; it's time to start putting things in to perspective. As aforementioned, before my new life, my first work experience had involved working with young people. As I began to step-up to the plate and refocus on my goals, I initiated contact with local youth organisations and eventually made contact with an organisation called "Inspirational youth."

Inspirational youth was the first organisation I became involved with, whose main focus was to assist young people in turning their lives around for the better. I had emailed the founder and managing director and we maintained contact via email and eventually I was invited to meet with them officially in person. As soon as I arrived, I was taken into a meeting room to discuss my plans. I was asked what I wanted to achieved and told them about my vision to change the world by representation within schools and my plans to offer mentoring sessions.

The Managing Director; was amazed by my drive and ambition and congratulated me on my efforts, whilst admitting it was unique to discuss such proposals with individuals within my age group. This meeting led to my first inspirational speech in front of three hundred graduates an event that had been organised in conjunction with Inspirational Youth. The Lambeth Mayor was also in attendance and his constituency. The talk I presented received a standing ovation from the audience, which resonated with me, bringing a tear to my eyes which I am able to sustain through "toxic masculinity" and I find myself instead laughing. I had no idea I had it within me to reach an audience in such an astounding way.

In an online post I wrote:

Deemed as an under achiever in school, constantly in the bottom set, but I was also a man with little self-esteem, unaware of my talents; let alone having the ability to inspire hundreds of people. It all started after I had made a life changing decision at the age of twenty-one I promised to make the rest of my life, the best of my life. This often still feels surreal at times but with Christ all things are possible. The main guest speaker at Lambeth college graduation that year was myself, Kevin Munga.

On the 19th of April 2017 Inspirational Youth posted in an article my mission statement:

Kevin Munga says "I am trying to challenge the ideology that in order to be "somebody" where I am from you need road status, and the only way young black males make it where I am from is if they know how to kick a ball or write lyrics." Kevin is heavily influenced by the likes of Martin Luther King Jr and Dr Myles Munroe. He says he respects their journeys and the fact they were world changers. When writing his first book "Young Black Males Have Potential," he believes society will change its opinion on how they view young black males, which will consequently bring about the change and will open many doors for these young men. He thinks this will be a positive incentive as it will enable other young men to live their lives to their full potential.

The beginning of something beautiful is to know my purpose which means there is no looking back.

Chapter fourteen ~ Lights, camera and action

Lights, camera and action after speaking at Lambeth College continued to speak at other events. Nevertheless, I knew real recognition would come from media outlets. I understood the importance of television interviews, radio stations and articles especially for the exposure of my first book "Young Black Males Have Potential," it was one of my prayers to have this type of reach. One fateful afternoon I received a call from the Croydon Advertiser they said I had been referred to them. My eyes lit up, I knew how many doors an article with my face featured on the cover would generate. The paper interviewed me and on the 29th of December 2017 I appeared in an article that headlined "The former Croydon gang member now studying to become a lawyer."

I was angered initially after reading the headline, because that was not what we had agreed prior to the article being published. I definitely did not agree to being referred to as a former gang member. In my mind, the headline should have stated "Young man from Croydon escapes gang life and now mentors young men away from gangs. Without any previous media experience, I had learnt the hard way. The first sentences of the article read "A former gang member of a Croydon gang whose teenage years were swallowed up by crime and violence has become an inspiration on the right side of law." At least they mentioned I had turned in to an inspiration; however the reference of my teenage years being swallowed up in crime, I felt was exaggerated.

I had never even been to prison before, however the article had portrayed me as one of the worst criminals known to society, in order to sell more copies. Disappointed with the outcome I completely understood the initial delay in making contact with a news outlet. This occurrence had certainly made me wiser when speaking to the media in future. Following the article, I did a lot more media and radio interviews online. Soon after this I was surprised by a Facebook message from a journalist at RT UK a Russian channel who stated "We've already brought your book!"

I replied to the message confirming my gratitude for their support. The journalist invites to the studio, although I am a little sceptical of the media, due to previous experience. I notice how keen the journalist is as she resorts to selling the benefits of being on the channel. I remember seeking my Mother's advice and she told me to "Go ahead, as long as you control the narrative you can control the conversation." Those were the words I needed to hear I agreed to appear on RT's TV station and they sent a car for me at five that evening. At one in the afternoon, I remember thinking man I needed a trim and ran to the barber-shop to get a fresh cut. At five, the car arrived on time and I was excited the car had been sent just for ME!

I reported to the main office of the television studios and was directed to go up the stairs. It felt weird being at a TV station. As I arrived on to the RT UK floor, I was escorted inside. Inside the studio I conversed with the interviewer and journalist prior to recording the show with the make-up crew busy in attendance. I noticed a copy of my book on a table and found it difficult to fathom that a TV station with an audience of over eight million viewers were familiar with my book and my work. The journalist began to interview me and I responded to the questions asked to the best of my ability. The interview had only lasted eight minutes, but felt like it had taken an eternity. After the interview the journalist suggested I should become their Gang consultant, due to the way I had successfully handled the interview.

I was pleased with the feedback I had received and thanked them for their hospitality whilst they removed the audio equipment. I returned home thereafter and waited to see the pre-recorded show. I watched the interview with my Mother who was proud of my efforts, little did I know this would be the first of many TV interviews to come. A few months later I received a call from someone I had met after an online interview. He asked how I was and introduced himself stating he was calling from television channel "London Live." They were doing a TV special called "Stephen Lawrence day" and were inviting me to attend as their special guest, I was honoured. I responded regretfully that I was unable to attend, due to a prior commitment. I had promised to take my younger cousin to a football match and I did not want to let him down. I was asked if I could make alternative arrangements, however it was impossible due to the short notice I had been given. I was aware of the major opportunity I was turning down, had I taken any other decision, would have meant disappointing my younger cousin which I didn't have the heart to do. I started making excuses in my head and decided the location of the studio was too far to get to, so I declined the kind offer. I knew God was watching; a few months later London Live called again for a special interview.

I still remember the television journalist introducing me on the program, like it was yesterday... "Lawyer Kevin Munga is helping other young Londoners turn their backs on violence and crime. He has a written a book "Young Black Males Have Potential." As the journalist spoke I reminisced how far I had come. I remember laughing to myself, that I had been introduced as a Lawyer, and had not qualified yet, however with graduating in Law and work experiences it was in the works. After the interview with London Live, I had additional interviews with the BBC and had been contacted by Sky News. The French media and Dutch National TV had also made contact. When I look at how far I have come since then, I can only praise God.

I had started meeting with people from within the media industry, following my TV appearance, including comedians and professional boxers, many of the personalities I had met were considered humble and inspiring. It was a really good feeling knowing it was achieveable in making it out a deprived area.

Getting a seat at the table with such ingenuity was possible even though, I came from outside of the entertainment industry.

Conversations with people from the industry opened my eyes, in particular one conversation specifically. I was conversing with a comedian who had a significant following, he told me he respected the work I was doing. I responded I held a great admiration for his craft and was amazed by the platform he had amassed. He said was appreciative of my response, but informed me that he was aware of my differences from other individuals like me and admired my decision to not conforming to the pitfalls of society. That day made me realise it's the differences that inspires others. There is no prerequisite to change your course because you think you will not get the accolades for what you do. You desire; credibility it can be obtained from within the path you choose. In addition, I also realised that a 'celebrity-status' is also non-contributing factor, the only requirement is to be credible or established in your chosen field.

Maybe if it does not exist yet, it is waiting for you to create it. – Eric Thomas.

Chapter fifteen ~ According to God's will

"Trust God not society"

I made the effort to trust God solely whenever it concerned family, friends or society. Not to say that individual advice is a bad thing. Guidance can be useful, but can also be arduous when considering the appropriate course of advice. Throughout the course of this journey, whilst the intensity of the media spotlight increases, there are some family members who have expressed concern that I may be taking on too much and have suggested I slow down. However, being in such an illustrious position has increased my understanding of the complex and often lengthy process involved in fulfilling my duty.

Friends and family often advise us on what we should do, what university degree we should study and what profession to choose. At times we even allow society to dictate what we should or shouldn't do. We have allowed society to define what beauty means to us. What shade of colour beauty is supposed to be and what texture of hair makes a woman beautiful. We are constantly bombarded via social media daily, informing us how we ought to live our lives from the insights of people we don't personally know and it is easy to become despondent by the false lifestyles being displayed across Social media platforms which precedes my next point. Following the media recognition I realised how important it was not to focus solely on social media. Additionally, if I ever wanted to solidify my legacy, I could do using a variety of social media platforms. I had an important message to administer and decided to record a live video, in order to create the right impact, the message was simple:

"Social media is an amazing platform, but it should not be the main and only platform that you are found on. You can either aspire to have a hundred thousand followers or for your work to be on billboards, in galleries, institutions or even incorporated in to curriculums." I started to realise many of us where doing things because that is what can gain us popularity. Quality and purpose is more desirable than popularity, it is not about doing what is popular, but about doing what is purposeful. We sometimes hold back from the truth, out of fear that it may be interpreted as controversial or unpopular. If you are unpopular telling the truth then so be it!

If you are meant to be popular it will happen organically. As I stuck to my principals and continued my journey, I became confident enough to reject instances that did not sit well with my spirit, regardless of how large the opportunities appeared. On one occasion I was sitting in my room and received a What's App message from a previous employer, the Director and Founder of Inspirational Youth. He asked me how I was doing, even though we no longer worked together, we had continued to maintain a good relationship. He mentioned the Mayor had invited me for a special knife crime event. Initially I thought he was referring to the local Croydon Mayor. Later I received the invitation by email and I notice it was the London Mayor Speech invitation. I recall my surprise thinking how surreal it was that the London Mayor even knew of my existence.

The event was all I had imagined it would be and more, I was even able to speak with the Mayor at the end of the event and gifted him a copy of my first book "Young Black Males Have Potential." We exchanged contacts and he to begin reading the book as soon as he returned to the office. Following that meeting I also had the fortune of meeting Jordan B Peterson, the renowned clinical psychologist and best-selling author. I found him to be very encouraging and told me to keep pushing forward. We discussed a range of topics including masculinity and intellectualism. I went from meeting people within the industry to meeting politicians, intellectuals and other authors. I had developed a keen sense of the types of meet-ups beneficial to my growth which leads me to my other point. At times we often dream about meeting famous celebrities that we are unable to identify with. It's important to research your chosen profession attempt to connect with those who are relatable to your field. I you do things according to God's Will the only acceptance that is required comes from Him.

Chapter sixteen ~ It is greater than you

With the experience I had gained, I began to market myself better, opportunities were multiplying, from speaking in schools and churches I was contacted to speak at an annual Christian camp. The Reaching Higher Limitless Christian camp, speaking with the Founder, he conveyed how valuable my presence would be at the event. I was surprised by his statement, because I was still unaware of my value at the time. Often we look in the mirror and only see the image in front of us, we frequently miss how the world views us. Still in shock that I have been requested to attend the event in the capacity of special guest speaker. The Founder had invited me to speak at the event and requests fifty copies of my books and we agree a booking fee. During the week of camp I made preparations to get myself ready to travel the 136 miles to attend the event; although nervous I felt privileged to be given the opportunity of inspiring hundreds of young teenagers.

The camp event is due to start on Monday and my slot had been arranged to take place the following day. So I make my way on the Tuesday on getting there I am greeted by a female representative who offers warm hospitality in making me feel welcomed. She shows me to my room, so I can settle in. Accompanied with my bible I set my suitcase down and say a little prayer, before leaving the room to get acquainted and meet the other leaders also in attendance. As I leave my room I notice how vast the venue was and the capacity it could hold.

It made me think about delivering a lecture as the main guest speaker. The service starts and the congregation begins to worship. I begin to pray "Lord take control, I don't even know what I am going to say; may the words I utter come solely from you." The host announces me up on to the stage and I begin my talk. I ensure God takes control; I engage with the audience by introducing myself and discussing elements of my upbringing, adversities and challenges I had experienced and the achievements I had gained as part of my transition and left them with a four-stage test. I dissected education into four components:

- Academia

- Vocation

- Knowledge

- Civilisation

As I end my speech by thanking the audience for taking the time to listen everyone applauds, including one of the leaders who proceeds to take the stage and we immediately enter into worship which evokes an outpouring of emotion from the audience members. As I leave the stage to head back to my own quarters, a woman stops me on the way and states she found my speech powerful.

The following day I was selected as a panellist for an event called "Brotherhood." The event was a secure venue for us to discuss toxic masculinity, struggles that men encounter growing up in inner-city London. I could see a few of the other characters also present in the room. Many questions were asked, but the recurring theme on how to stay remain focused without becoming distracted.

"How does one look at the bigger picture and strive towards their goal despite the adversity?" I didn't have the opportunity to reply at the time of the original discussion; however I am able to provide my response here. It is imperative the main focus is centered on the purpose of the goal. Is the intent based on selfish desire or for the betterment of another? Secondly, you should consider the response that you would like to achieve following any success. Does success retain its value, if none of your friends or no one is aware of your work? Consider the possibilities of your success being recognised internationally and the impact on these individuals, as a result. Sometimes we don't want success for the greater good and any gains are used as a means of demonstrating to others that we are doing well.

On the Friday I had left camp having made a valued acquaintance, the host who had welcomed me to the event earlier. She went out of her way to ensure I was okay, during my stay and we are still in contact today, CA as she prefers to be known. Leaving the camp, I realised how many young people had been impacted by my story. I had completed a large book signing which I consider the most poignant days of my life, seeing so many young black men from similar walks of life queue for a copy of my book. The books were becoming as popular as the latest mixtapes in circulation. At that point, the mission felt like it was definitely working; however it was just the beginning of things to come.

A month later I had planned a trip to the Democratic Republic of Congo, my place of origin. I had been working hard to help turn around the lives of youth offenders in the UK for the previous three to four years and felt the time was right to carry out such an initiative, to the motherland. On my arrival to the Democratic Republic of Congo I feel a sense of cautiousness as I had been warned about the greed back home. As I get off the plane I am met by a police officer, he has been sent to collect me from the plane. He addresses me by name, which takes me aback and explains my cousin has sent him to escort me and that a driver and my mother were waiting for me. I was excited, I hadn't been back home since the age of two, little did I know that immediately stepping off that plane I would experience the "Congolese greed." I walked past the first security guard without incident, but upon my approach towards the exit I was stopped by a second security guard who had been observing me.

I asked the police officer why I was being detained and he explained the guard wanted to check my vaccination certificate, which I duly handed to him, and although it was valid he insisted I paid sixty dollars. The police officer I was with was upset for me and explained to the guard that it was my first visit back home. "How bad does it look, he's only just entered in to the country and he is already being bribed for money?" The guard apologised and added he was supposed to obtain his vaccination fifteen days before arrival, but the certificates states it was done just five days before. The police officer gave the guard twenty dollars adding "He will not pay more than that" as he handed him the money. The guard reluctantly accepted the funds and allowed us to exit the airport. On our way out I could hear the familiar Lingala dialect, I felt the heat and instantly felt at home, especially after being reunited with my Mother.

Making our way to the car from the airport everyone seemed to be "my family" I noticed a young man had grabbed my luggage from my hands and referred to us as "cousins." My Mum told me not to pay the gesture any mind because they will say or do anything for a dollar. I felt dejected by the façade, being reminded first-hand of the stereotypical portrayals of Africa. I been to Nigeria before, but nevertheless it was still overly painful to witness. I was about to hand the vagrant some of money, but my mother looked at me and remonstrated "If you start giving them money from the airport, you will be left with nothing by the time we leave here." When we arrived at the apartment we had rented we were approached by some workers at the gate who enquired with my Mother ("Mere mwana nayo?") whether I was her son, which she instantly confirmed.

The following morning, I woke up keen and ready to see the entire city. I had woken up early and went to take a shower soon after realising that the water was stone cold. I showered in the cold water with the use of a bucket which proved to be a humbling experience.

Meeting the Mungas

Shortly after my arrival, word had quickly spread I was in town, some remembered me as baby Michael and had not seen me since I was two. My cousin came to me at the apartment and we were on our way to see the family. He was keen for us to begin he drive early, so I would able to meet as many people as possible. I began mentally preparing myself for the long day my cousin anticipated it would be and understood the importance of family, soon after I would be reunited with long-lost uncles, aunts and cousins. By the end of the day I felt completely exhausted and this had only been my first full day back, on the Sunday of that week one of my Mother's friends came to meet us to attend church.

I loved it; church was amazing the congregation was friendly and seemed grateful for life, it really made me realise how inappreciative individuals were in the western world by comparison. I left church and went straight to the barbers for the fresh haircut. The barbers had a good reputation for trimming hair, after my haircut I paid double the price. I did so because I could not comprehend how little they were being rewarded (the realities of Africa). After visiting one of my Father's sisters and an older cousin of mine, we discussed my plan to execute my vision to decrease youth violence in the Democratic Republic of Congo.

They are interested in my concepts, and my Aunt suggests going on TV to present my vision and introduce my book and inquire whether the opportunity would be possible. My Aunt states one of the main journalists at RTNC National Congolese TV is a good friend of hers. She made contact with them and made an appointment. It was a requirement to attend an interview beforehand to ascertain whether I was going to discuss anything controversial. For example, referring to the President in a negative manner, freedom of speech in the DRC is almost none-existent; I already knew what I had planned to say would be welcomed by God's grace. I completed the interview with the journalist and the date of the programme going to air was set and would be on TV the Wednesday of that week.

With my speech prepared I knew what I wanted to talk about and how I wanted it to come across. On the way to the TV studios we were involved in a car crash. It felt surreal the incident had occurred on the way to my Congolese TV debut. We were able to reach an agreement and go our separate ways with the person we had crashed in to and continued on our way. I entered the building and was ushered in to the studio and within five, four three, two; one I found myself live on National Television and the host was in the throes of presenting me to the programme "Activist and author Kevin Munga has joined us in the studio to discuss his book with us." The presenter asked various questions and asked about my mission. My message was simple:

"For more than two years prior to this interview, social change has been my priority, people are my priority. No funding no resources just a pen and a voice that the Lord has been using I had been given a French passport at birth; however my heart says I am Congolese. The youth of Congo have potential.

Despite the various problems.

Despite the adversity.

Despite the poverty.

You are not Kuluna's (gangsters) you are not Shegue's" (street kids).

My Mission:

It is important for individuals to integrate in to an established society, in order to create opportunities (careers), rehabilitation and eradication of labels. Following the interview, I left the TV studio and returned home and waited for the programme to air on TV, due to being pre-recorded. As the programme aired and I saw myself being introduced, my heart began to pulsate quickly. I felt a little nervous to see how I appeared on TV and secondly I was excited about my message of hope being broadcasted. As I watched my message across the screen, I started to receive an outpouring of messages from members of my family sharing how proud they were of me. I logged on to my Facebook and viewed an influx of messages from other provinces, even from people in other African countries such as Angola.

I knew that this was the beginning of something meaningful and for the rest of my stay I felt encouraged to continue with the vision. However, my encounters with the Congolese mentality continued to conflict. I was working with individuals people who were not as committed. I envisioned starting my mission with a campaign to include bill boards with my slogan stating, "Congolese youth have potential," but I kept receiving false promises. I felt despondent, but I knew that the interview would end up in the archives and one day I would be able to fulfil my Congolese dreams.

One the day of my departure to the UK, it was time to say goodbye to my family members and the many friends I had made during my time there. I wanted to give everyone something as I was leaving, but unfortunately I did not have the means to. I was able to give what I could to some of the workers I met and offer consoling words of comfort to others. The ride to the airport was a bitter-sweet moment and felt as if I could have done more. As I passed through the security clearance my mother who was to remain in the Congo said her farewells.

Waiting at boarding gates I found myself seated next to another traveller, who sparked a conversation with me. He told me that it was his first time travelling to Europe and he wasn't sure if he was sitting at the correct terminal. I was able to reassure him that he was and discussed the purpose of his travel. The gentleman was due to attend an important conference with other MP's and Ministers. I asked him about his position and he confirmed he was an Honourable MP. We ended up discussing my mission and how I had been disappointed I had been unable to do more during my visit.

The MP offered to help with my plans and offered me the use of his resources. We exchanged contact and continued on our travels as I made myself comfortable inside the aircraft I felt an emotion of satisfaction, knowing my Congolese dream could soon come to fruition. I reminisced on the plane and started thinking about my time in the Congo. Returning to the UK I realised that I had fallen in my love with my country during my first visit and knew that my first visit, would by no means be my last, by God's grace. As an admirer of the country, I felt compelled to compose a letter to my beloved nation.

Chapter seventeen ~ Letter to the Democratic Republic of Congo

Dear Congo,

In a country where the average yearly wage of citizens can be as little as $394.25, which is in sharp contrast in comparison to a country such as Qatar, whereby people earn on average $105.091.42. In a country where there is uncertainty and the disparities between the rich and the poor are immense. In a country where when your Congolese brethren says Monday it really means Wednesday laugh out loud. I come from a country rich in minerals (cobalt, coltan and copper), however showering with hot water is considered a luxury. From a country where the minerals that sources your mobile is also responsible for fuelling endless violence; from a country where children are not going to school because of a lack of finance. Young men who are struggling to make ends meet are labelled as Kulana's (gangsters) and Shegue's (street kids). In a country where young men and women study diligently to become lawyers and doctors, remain unemployed for years or when they eventually find employment are underpaid; in a country where there is a church on every corner because Jesus equals hope.

Dear Congo, I love you and I know better days are coming.

Yours Sincerely,

Kevin Munga

Chapter eighteen ~ Purpose in prayer

"Back to purpose, but not back to reality"

Many times I realised when people would be back from abroad "say back to reality," completely unaware that once you are living your purpose your reality cannot be attributed to something negative. Therefore, if you imply the term "back to reality," it can only be interpreted in a positive way.

When you've been made to feel inadequate in the past, the moment you are able to change your circumstances and begin to lead a purposeful life, it begins to alter the trajectory of your life. You automatically fear ever feeling inadequate again. That fear is an amazing reminder of your mission wherever you go. You are literally made to feel unstable when you are not working. The mentoring starts, I had received a message from a local woman seeking mentoring; I responded to her message confirming unfortunately I was not in a position to provide mentoring services at that time. Due to not having the proper facilities in place to assist with her son's care order.

She told me it would be of great comfort if I was able to speak to her son, I also sensed the urge to take him out for something to eat and to meet him. I was able to speak with him in person and gain an insight into some of the challenges he faced, after taking him back to his Mothers, she was grateful for my time and we remained in contact till this day. The mother tells her son to consider myself as family and informs me that a woman from the youth offending service, has been purchasing copies of my books and donating them to the local police stations, in the hope that my story will change even one person's life. I felt so empowered by what she had told me, she was able to restore my hope and reignite the purpose of my mission.

I realised that I did not need to chase "fame" for my message o be transmitted; all I required was the correct recognition. I had eceived a second call soon after from a school in North London, Forstimere Sixth Forth they had requested me to attend and omplete a book-signing at the school for Black History month. As I arrived at the school, every student turned out to greet me and was overwhelmed with the turnout. "Mr Kevin Munga we have heard so much about you, our teacher always talks about you", the tudent told me. I was thinking about my life and how far I had come.

What were the odds? I was not a footballer or a rapper; however every single student knew of my existence. Alternative treated, young plumbers, authors, pilots, electricians will begin getting the recognition they deserve for the amazing work they do, here is no room for anymore unsung heroes. I started to realise he importance of my message, I had come up with a plan which ater transformed into a mission inspired by Kevin Munga. The program included free books of "Young Black Males Have Potential" followed by my testimonial, I began to be contacted by chools located in other cities and they updated me about their plans to incorporate the book in to their school curriculums. Wow! I was blown away with such positive responses and started o see how far 'we' had come along on this journey. I say 'we' because the mission is far bigger than me. One day I was considered just a young man who came from a deprived background, however I am able to confidently state if Kevin Munga can do it, then surely you can.

I remember reviewing my vision board and noticed I was on rack, but there was one thing missing, I had not had the opportunity to speak at a prison yet.

Cleary God listens to prayer and just a few days later I received a call inviting me to speak at HMP Wandsworth prison or Black History month. On the day of the visit I got dressed that morning, after praying, before setting on my way to speak at the prison. I found it hard to convey my feelings. I was going to speak at an adult prison, I felt excited and nervous at the same time. I had concerns about being able to motivate individuals from within the confined facility. Now when I think about it the answer stood out right in front of me. Trust in the Lord with all thine heart; and lean not unto thine own understanding – Proverbs3.5 In all thy ways acknowledge Him, and He shall direct thy paths. I gave my speech to God and asked Him to speak through me; the experience was amazing and opened my eyes to many things.

I took to my social media platform and wrote on my status:

"Inspired by these inmates, I got asked some very intelligen questions.

Prison is not about the four walls man! Prison is a state of mind You have incarcerates in there who think better than those who have freedom.

Thank you for having me HM Prison Wandsworth.

Young Black Males Have Potential - the book is now available in the prison's library. We've come a long way; however there is stil a very long way to go.

Spoke to a lifer who said he could relate to me. Spoke to another inmate who wants to write a book; the opportunities are endless Do not ever hold your tongue you do not know who you can save and touch through your message."

After my speech at the prison I received a message from my close friend TR, he said BUN Wandsworth, I hate that jail I jus replied with LOL. Regular conversations with him TR had always been a real character, shortly after that he sent another message using my old alias "No Manners Drillz," How do you expect to have manners? This guy was always cracking me up man, little did I know this would be the very last message he would ever send to me.

TR's death

I received a message February 2020 from a friend of mine asking if I had heard the news. I replied heard what? Without waiting for a response I exited Whats app and typed "Croydon stabbing" into the Google search bar; another crazy reality. You are reading this probably thinking why did I think of the worse? The people you grow up with where I'm from often turn into distant memories. I was shaking I went back onto Whats app; I knew for a fact that particular friend would not message me for no reason. I asked K, what happened? She replied I am sorry, TR died last night. I was hoping you would have heard, I am sorry that I had to be the bearer of bad news. I am at work trying to hold it together and fighting back the tears. I arranged with her to contact me whilst I was moving home.

When K called I could her hear sobbing on the phone "He was stabbed six times." I told her I would call back after she finished work. It took me a while to process what I had just heard, I broke down crying. Even as I write about it now, I still get the chills. TR, How? Lord why? He was an amazing soul. Once again the "Ends" strike. I remember speaking to him whilst I was in University and he was in Prison crazy, it sounds like there is a thin line between University and Prison where I am from. I recalled a previous incident on the train; I had gotten into a fight and TR had my back, I remembered the times he would call out "Croydon President." He believed in me, he made me laugh so much; I couldn't fathom how we could lose such an amazing soul. TR was always smiling, I had never seen him sad, and he was generous and extremely humorous at times. However, here I was standing in front of his picture at his nine-night broken, holding my cousin and friend. Whilst everyone is talking revenge, how could we not want to get revenge for him?

After a few days I felt God's peace come upon me.

I was ready to roll with Christ this was another wakeup call tomorrow's not promised. Inky Johnson states if this was the last week of your life how would you live it? How would you treat your family? How would you serve? These rhetorical questions keep repeating in my head, so I go to church by this time I had not been to church in a while. I was praying at home but I knew about the importance of gatherings. For where two or three are gathered in my Name, there I am among them – Matthew 18:20. As I go to ARC Church I find myself falling to my knees my life is not my own, but God's TR is Gone, AL is gone and MO is gone, yet I am living and breathing by your grace only.

A few months later I find myself talking with family members debating on God's existence. We spoke about many things, whether contradiction exists in the bible? The God (Jesus) depicted with the blue-eyed images we see on TV is definitely not how Jesus looks. There were many raising logic rather than facts and history. Knowing the many challenges I have experienced there is nothing that will be able to convince me that God is non-existence.

After explaining it in an intellectual way for a couple of hours, whilst subjectively debating. My counter argument remained simple. "Experience is subjective you are entitled to have your own beliefs and to maintain strong convictions about them. In my case, the love of Christ is the path I chose to follow for the rest of my life.

Protect your faith and guard your hearts.

Chapter nineteen ~ Letter to my readers

Dear Readers,

Who are you? You are beautiful and wonderfully made and courageously created in God's image, full of purpose and special. God knows the exact amount of hairs adorned on your head. He knows your five year plan and even your ten year plan; He knows what your next minute entails. He knows why certain things are not working just yet and how much growth you need to complete, before the door you are patiently waiting for finally unlocks. Do what feels natural, don't conform to society's perspectives and be true to yourself. Don't embed your individuality in to things that you would like to acquire, whether you acquire it or not you are still YOU and that's your power. Everything happens for a reason, so trust the process there are no coincidences, have faith.

Yours Sincerely,

Kevin Munga

Bonus Chapter (Quotes)

Quotes written by Kevin Munga.

"The effect you have on others is the most valuable currency here is."

"If you can control yourself with alcohol, women, drugs many other things you automatically take control of your life. Discipline is not restriction it is freedom.

"The more discipline the greater the probability to tap into what God has predestined for you."

"Education is not just attending an institution it is much more than that. Education is being the recipient of anything has to do with systematic instruction plus more. Education is survival."

"Success is expensive, and the currency is sacrifice".

"Whenever you feel down just remember five years ago you never thought you would be the person you are today. Hold your head up, slow progress is better than no progress."

"Integrity has a cost".

-"Aim to impact lives to a point that, when you are no more we almost forget that you are gone. Because we can see you through your work.

-"You do not need to be a celebrity. You just need to be known or credible in your field of work."

- "You want to know how restricted human beings are, go to a funeral. Everyone is crying however no one can do a thing. Stop worshipping men of God, public figures and celebrities start worshiping the Lord.

- "Culture often brings people together this translates into love, tradition and solidarity. However we have been in many environments which could be deemed as uncultured due to lack of Morality."

-"Human being are limited so I plugged into a higher being Jesus Christ."

-"It is not mandatory to give your children what you did not have growing up. However it is mandatory to teach them what you did not know growing up."

- "Every decision helps construct or destroy this one life."

-"In life 95% of the time there's no right answer. So make you sure you look at things from different angles."

-"The only thing that is constant is change, embrace it."

-"Experience is subjective, you may see one thing whereas

-"You do not chase the position, you chase the goal then the position chases you."

-"If most people knew who they were they would drop a lot of the habits they have now."

-"What are we if not our stories."

-"You do not wait for people to get big to start supporting them that is too easy."

-"We are all running away from something or running towards something. Make sure you are running in the right direction (your purpose."

-"Two stage test

A.) If it is detrimental to your calling.

       Or

B.) Having an adverse effect on your well-being.

Separate yourself from it."

-"If he is black and well-spoken he sounds white, ignorance."

-"It will happen organically just be humble, genuine and deliberate."

-"Intellectual weaponry is a necessity or they will never take us seriously."

-"Speaking is good, exemplifying is better."

Reasons for writing this book

Kevin Munga is heavily influenced by the likes of Dr Myles Munroe and Dr Martin Luther King. Whilst listening to a Dr Myles Munroe sermon the topic focused on discovering who you are and realising your purpose on Earth.

Inspired by the lesson, Kevin turned his abilities to discovering his true purpose. Realising the challenges in his life has happened, in order to define the man he has become today. Following that epiphany, Kevin is keen to share his insights with others who are interested in learning the key principals of self-identity and related issues contained within this book.

Acknowledgements

I would like to thank the Munga and Kasumbi family who have helped me become the man I am today.

I would like to thank my Aunt Mireille Feza and Uncle Mira Mutombo for being big supporters.

My cousins Grand Abdon Munga and Olivier Tshikumbi for being massive supporters.

Eliane Palhinhas for her consistent support.

Lydia Mumba for her consistent support.

My Mother Scholastique Ngalula for her consistent support.

S. Lewis-Campbell, SLC Publishing contact: slcpublishing@icloud.com (editorial services and support)

Finally, I would like to thank those who continue to support my work.

Contact:

Instagram: @Kevinmunga_

Snapchat: Kevinspires1

Facebook: Kevin Munga

Printed by Amazon Italia Logistica S.r.l.
Torrazza Piemonte (TO), Italy

13181073R00051